THE GHOST IN THE MIRROR

Karen Dolby

Illustrated by Brenda Haw

Designed by Kim Blundell and Brian Robertson

Series Editor: Gaby Waters

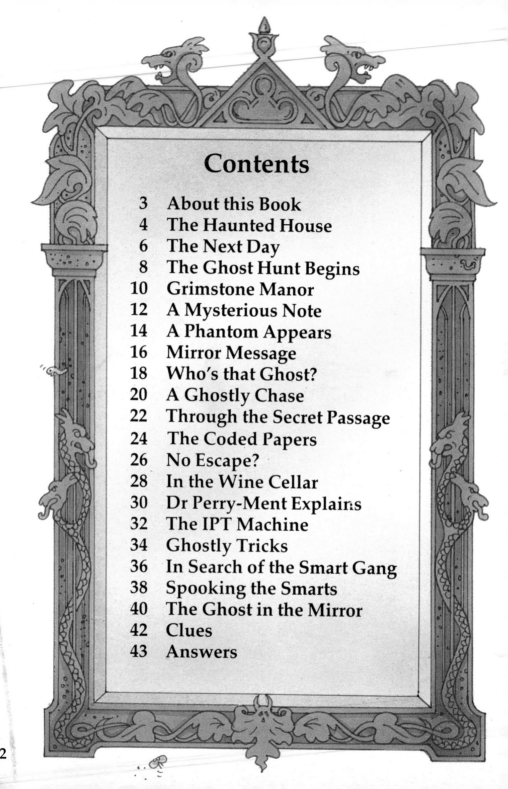

Contents

About this Book

The Ghost in the Mirror is a spooky adventure story with a difference. The difference is that you can take part in the adventure.

Throughout the book, there are lots of ghostly puzzles and perplexing problems which you must solve in order to understand the next part of the story.

Look at the pictures carefully and watch out for vital clues. Sometimes you will need to flip back through the book to help you find an answer. There are extra clues on page 42 and you can check the answers on pages 43 to 48.

Just turn the page to begin the adventure.

Sam, Joe and Polly were on their way home from school late one Friday evening. The gates to Grimstone Park were always locked, but this evening the gates are open. Should they go in? Sam leads the way…

GRIM STONE PARK

Polly

Joe

Sam

The Haunted House

Joe, Polly and Sam scuffed their way through the park, drawing closer and closer to Grimstone Manor. The house loomed dark and menacing above the trees.

"Here's the haunted house," Sam joked.

Joe peered through the gates. He had never been so close to the Manor before. Suddenly, an eerie green light glowed through one of the windows. Sam froze in horror as a flickering shadow appeared briefly at the window.

"There's probably someone living there now," Polly gulped.

"But the house has been empty for years," said Sam.

An owl hooted suddenly. Polly shivered. Grimstone Manor looked very mysterious. Sam's teeth chattered. He was convinced the house was haunted. But Joe was sure there was another explanation and wanted to investigate.

He stared up at the Manor. It was dark and creepy; the gates were locked; they didn't even have a flashlight. Perhaps it wasn't such a good idea.

"We'll come back first thing tomorrow," he said, finally.

The Next Day

Joe led the way back to Grimstone Manor, itching to begin the ghost hunt. Sam and Polly followed, struggling to keep up.

"Hide!" Joe whispered suddenly.

He pointed at two odd-looking people lounging against the wall ahead, talking in low voices. He didn't want anyone to see them sneaking around the house.

As they ducked behind some bushes, Sam tripped and dived head first through a small hole in the wall.

Polly and Joe crawled through after him and found themselves staring up at Grimstone Manor. In the daylight it looked empty and neglected and not at all scary. Joe marched up to one of the roughly boarded windows and tugged hard at a sheet of corrugated iron.

He quickly tried the others and groaned. They were securely nailed down and windows that had been left unboarded, were blocked by trash. He stared at the house and in a flash, saw how they could get in.

Can you find a way in?

The Ghost Hunt Begins

Polly and Joe were soon inside. Sam had more trouble. Joe looped one end of the rope around the bannister rail and pulled. Sam grabbed the pole and Polly tried to haul him in. But Sam remained outside, dangling in midair. He was stuck between the two halves of the window and didn't dare look down.

At last they succeeded. Sam fell in and landed with a bump. He began to wonder if a ghost hunt was worth so much effort. But Joe was already thinking about where to start. It was a large, rambling house. How would they find their way around? The stairs going up were rotten and had collapsed, so they had no choice but to go down first.

Polly and Joe stared through the open door at a crumbling, cobwebby room which used to be a gift shop. The house had been open to the public once.

"It looks as if no one's been here for years," said Polly, venturing inside.

Suddenly she saw something that would be very helpful.

What has Polly spotted?

Grimstone Manor

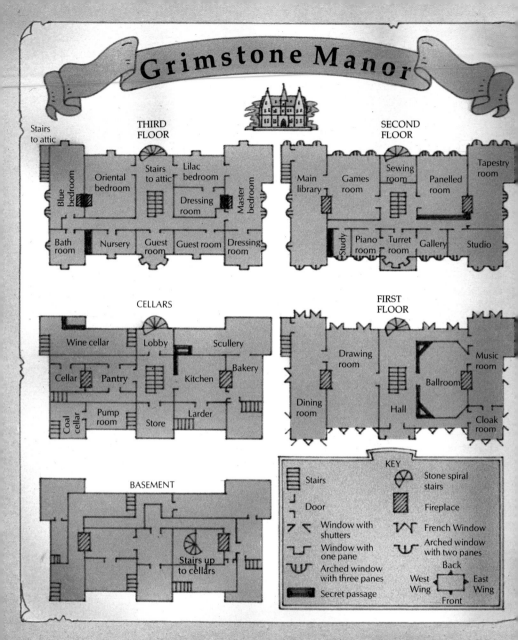

THIRD FLOOR

Stairs to attic

Blue bedroom | Oriental bedroom | Stairs to attic | Lilac bedroom | Dressing room | Master bedroom

Bath room | Nursery | Guest room | Guest room | Dressing room

SECOND FLOOR

Main library | Games room | Sewing room | Panelled room | Tapestry room

Study | Piano room | Turret | Gallery | Studio

CELLARS

Wine cellar | Lobby | Scullery

Cellar | Pantry | Kitchen | Bakery

Coal cellar | Pump room | Store | Larder

FIRST FLOOR

Drawing room | Music room

Dining room | Hall | Ballroom | Cloak room

BASEMENT

Stairs up to cellars

KEY

	Stairs		Stone spiral stairs
	Door		Fireplace
	Window with shutters		French Window
	Window with one pane		Arched window with two panes
	Arched window with three panes		
	Secret passage		

West Wing | Back | East Wing

Front

Sam read the short history of Grimstone Manor, shivering at the thought of strange lights, ghostly monks and secret passages.

He glanced around nervously expecting a ghastly ghost to appear at any minute.

"Where shall we go?" he asked.

10

Owners of Grimstone Manor

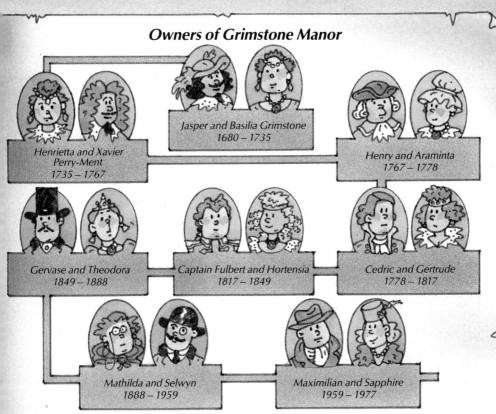

Jasper and Basilia Grimstone
1680 – 1735

Henrietta and Xavier Perry-Ment
1735 – 1767

Henry and Araminta
1767 – 1778

Gervase and Theodora
1849 – 1888

Captain Fulbert and Hortensia
1817 – 1849

Cedric and Gertrude
1778 – 1817

Mathilda and Selwyn
1888 – 1959

Maximilian and Sapphire
1959 – 1977

Grimstone Manor was built in 1680 by Jasper Grimstone. His only daughter, Henrietta, and her husband, Xavier Perrier-Mente, inherited the Manor in 1735. From that time, the house has been owned by the Perry-Ment family who have been known as the Counts and Countesses of Grimstone, since Captain Fulbert won the title for outstanding bravery. An inventive streak has always run through the Perry-Ments. While experimenting with gunpowder in 1862, Gervase blew up the East Wing and ballroom. These were later rebuilt by the brilliant architects, Sir John Truckbrugh and Sir Nicholas Hawksless.

The building itself is very mysterious. The thick walls hide secret passages and small rooms. There are also several secret and well-hidden doors with tricky, mechanical locks.

The Manor has more than its share of ghosts. It is supposed to be built on the site of a medieval priory and is said to be haunted by a spectral monk whose appearance is linked to strange, flashing lights. Visitors to the house have complained of sudden icy breezes, spooky noises and ghostly laughter.

"To the room with the flashing lights, of course," said Polly.

She studied the floor plans and thought back to last night.

She tried to picture the front of the house and soon knew exactly where they had to go.

Which room should they go to?

A Mysterious Note

When they reached the study, the heavy door creaked open. Polly, Joe and Sam peered in uncertainly wondering what to expect.

"Someone's been in here," said Polly, pointing at the thick dust on the floor. "Ghosts don't leave footprints."

Feeling bolder, they began looking around. The room was disappointingly normal and there was no trace of anything ghostly.

It was hard to imagine the strange, glowing light and mysterious, shadowy figure they had seen from outside.

12

Sam picked up a curious-looking book lying on the armchair and flicked through. It was very old.

"'Ancient Scientific Experiments that didn't Work'," he said, reading the title aloud.

As Joe glanced at the book, something else caught his eye.

Next to a dusty pile of books on the desk was a sheet of paper from a notebook. It was covered with writing and at first Joe thought it was written in a strange language. But as he looked more closely, he realized it was in code.

Can you decode the writing?

Rebmemer

ssap lliw uoy neht dna
elcric eht no sgyj eht
ecalp ssalg a yb elttob a
ton elttob a no ssalg a
erom on teg lliw uoy
ro nwod thgir hsup
rood eht rof sserp dna
eniw eht rof sserp
reillem eht tuo ekat
dna selttob eht rof kool
rallec terces ym ot
krad eht morf og ot

13

A Phantom Appears

Even decoded, the note didn't make any sense. It was definitely human, but it just added to the mystery.

Joe looked up, gulped and grabbed Polly's arm.

"Look . . ." he gasped, turning a strange color.

There, in the mirror was a terrible, ghostly apparition. Its face was shrouded, but Sam was sure it was staring at him.

"Let me out of here," he yelled, petrified.

A sudden, icy blast whistled through the room.

SLAM. Sam reached the door as it banged shut. There was a loud click and the latch dropped down on the other side, securely locking the door.

They were trapped in a haunted room. Polly stared into the mirror. The ghost had vanished, but who knew when it might return?

Sam hollered and tugged at the door, but it was no use. Joe rushed to the window. Feeling silly, he realized they were too high up to jump.

Meanwhile, Polly was thinking hard. There was something very peculiar about the large footprints on the dusty floor. They went in one direction only. The more she thought, the more sure she was.

"There's a secret door," she exclaimed, at last. "I know how we can get out."

Where is the secret door? How can they open it?

Mirror Message

The bookcase swung open just like a normal door, revealing a flight of stone steps going up. They ran to a small landing at the top and Joe cautiously pulled the red lever in front of him. A panel halfway up the wall slid aside and they climbed out into an old nursery.

Polly rubbed her eyes. The wooden horse in the middle of the room was rocking to and fro.

"There must be a draft," she muttered.

Sam wasn't sure, but he thought the door opposite had just closed quietly. And weren't those footsteps fading into the distance? He jumped as laughter echoed around the house.

"It's the wind," said Joe, sensibly.

Just then, Sam shrieked and made a dash for the door. He had caught sight of a mirror. There was something in it…

"Come back," called Polly. "It's only writing."

Joe was already studying the mirror. He could see the outline of words written in the cobwebby dust, but they didn't seem to make any sense.

"It's another code," exclaimed Polly.

What is written on the mirror?

Who's that Ghost?

It was very puzzling. The note in the study and the mirror message were definitely NOT ghostly, but what about the figure in the mirror and the strange noises? And what about the creepy feeling they each had that they were being watched? As they stepped out into the corridor, the nursery door slammed shut behind them.

"I wonder what we'll find?" Polly said, nervously.

Almost before she finished speaking, she heard a low, wailing sound. It grew louder and louder, and closer and closer. Finally, a white, shrouded figure appeared, blocking the corridor ahead. It seemed to float towards them, howling horribly.

"It's the phantom!" Sam yelled.

Polly's knees turned to jelly, but Joe wasn't scared.

"You're no ghost," he shouted. "You don't frighten me."

**Is Joe right?
What has he seen?**

A Ghostly Chase

Joe dashed after the imposter with Polly and Sam hot on his heels. They skidded around a corner in time to see the ghost nipping into a doorway ahead. They ran into a large bedroom after him and stopped. Where was the ghost? Polly looked under the bed, while Joe checked a chest and Sam peered into an enormous wardrobe.

"Over here," he shouted. "It's a door to the next room."

The three climbed through the deep, empty wardrobe into a small bedroom. The white figure glanced back at them and made a hasty exit. Joe, Polly and Sam raced after him and saw the ghost trip over his sheet and fall downstairs.

They followed the ghost into a small room. This time he was trapped. There was nowhere to hide. Suddenly, they were plunged into darkness. Polly flicked on her pocket flashlight, but the ghost had vanished.

"How did he do that?" asked Sam. "We were blocking the door."

"There must be another secret door," said Polly. "But where?"

Polly thought hard. She was sure something was different. But what was it? If only she knew, it might give them a clue.

What is different?
Where is the secret door?

Through the Secret Passage

Polly had a hunch. She tugged at the silk bell pull, sure it would open the panel. They watched open-mouthed as the fireplace and part of the wall began turning slowly. Halfway round they saw the other, almost identical fireplace swinging into the room.

"Come on," Joe shouted, jumping onto the grate.

The fireplace jolted to a stop in a wide passage. Joe briskly led the way forward. Polly held the flashlight.

There were strange scuttling noises, loud dripping and their footsteps echoed loudly. Every sound was magnified and it was also very dark. Their flashlight beam barely pierced the blackness as they crept gingerly down a flight of slippery, stone steps.

"I don't like this," groaned Sam, fighting his way through a cobweb with a rat scuttling across one foot.

Polly had to admit she was feeling a bit spooked and even Joe jumped when he came face to face with a glowing skull leering horribly at him. Finally, they stumbled down a second flight of steps into a narrow bedroom.

There was no sign of the ghost, but there were two small pinpoints of light halfway up the wall. Joe took the first turn to look through the spyholes and peered into a kitchen. He gulped, scarcely believing his eyes.

In a dusty, mirror, he saw the ghostly figure from the study. It seemed to stare through him. He could have been mistaken, but before it faded away, Joe was sure it made a sign as if warning him to be quiet.

The Boss will be pleased with the plan we've stolen.

Mmm… But we've still got to find the Doc and his secret laboratory, Rex.

Immediately, two people walked into the kitchen and Sam replaced Joe. He frowned as he heard snippets of their conversation. What were they up to?

We've seen that girl before," Polly gasped, taking her turn at the spyholes. "But where?"

Where have they seen the girl?

The Coded Papers

As soon as the sinister duo had gone, Sam yanked an old white lever high up in a beam. There was a loud CLICK. A panel sprang open and promptly shut as they climbed through.

"Look," said Polly, running into the room. "They've left this behind."

An official-looking file was lying on the table. Feeling a bit guilty, and making sure they really were alone, they quickly opened it.

Inside, there were two typed sheets, masses of photographs of the same person and a yellow, blue-print plan.

"This might tell us what's going on," said Joe, "… if only we could read it."

Most of the writing was in an impossible-looking code. Polly scratched her head and studied the words. Perhaps it wasn't so tricky after all.

Can you decode the writing?

TMARS GANG ROSSIED 2

Sang'g sseu rof eht eachinem:

doulc eb denter ot
rtheo srookc;
yntre ot kanb saultv,
suseumm dna
sallerieg (dna kuicq
sxite hitw tool
geavinl on eract);
yntre ot tovernmeng
sfficeo.

Nperatioo Yerrp-Tenm
sommencec 02:01
sourh no Yaturdas 42
Reptembes.

Eodc T

THE
BOSS

special nail
from IPT

OTHE CSMA ARTGA HNGDOSS
XIER1

EFACTS SKNO OWN

SNA CME: ODR EXAVIER
OPER ERY-EMENT

EBORN: 34 DDECEM
EBER 11950

Amoved sintogri emston zemanor din bearl
nysep etem cber. Mun oders nmart og xang
wsurve dilla ence isin qce 210 yse optem
hber. Bwo arld jfam kous tscien atist zwor
oking con ptopsec xre ftinve ention –
linstant wphysi dcal ptrans efer dence
imach tine. Dusesh tisown uspec tialc modet
fowor dkthem fach xinein ewhi
ich hsym ibols sequald tigits
40-9. Wsmar ots astil olwork
sing etobre vakc mode. Jhe tals
mosomet nimes luses oawo
erdcode efo hrh xis pnotes.

Scod bek

vital IPT
cog

25

No Escape?

Sam, Joe and Olly flipped through the rest of the papers and photos.

"This must be Dr X. Perry-Ment," said Joe, holding up one of the prints.

"And this is a plan of part of his invention," Sam added. "I wonder what it does?"

More importantly, WHO was Dr X. Perry-Ment and why was the Smart Gang looking for him?

"It's up to us to find some answers," said Joe. "I'm sure that creepy duo are up to no good. There's something fishy going on."

But there was no time to sit and wonder what.

Polly heard voices growing louder. The Smarts were returning! Sam and Joe fumbled frantically with papers and photos, desperately trying to cram them back into the file. Polly began looking for a way out.

Joe ran to the secret door. But there was no lever to open it from this side.

Polly opened the door from the bakery, only to find the steps were rotten.

Sam tugged frantically at the pantry door but it was locked and wouldn't budge.

Polly thought of the scullery but there was nowhere to hide or escape to in there. Just in time, they dived for cover in the only place they could see to hide. Heavy footsteps stomped into the room.

Silently, Joe pulled out the guidebook and map. There MUST be another way out... and they had to find it, fast.

Can you find another way out of the kitchen?

In the Wine Cellar

While the duo searched the bakery, Joe heaved open the trapdoor. They jumped down onto the flight of stone steps below and Sam shut the door before the crooks returned.

They ran through a maze of dark passages until they reached the large wine cellar below the dining room. A strange green glow shone through what seemed to be a solid wall. It reminded Joe of the flashes they had seen the night before. The glow traced the outline of a door. Could it be another secret entrance and the way in to the Doctor's laboratory? Joe tapped the wall lightly.

Sam wondered if it was such a good idea to try to get in. But if the creepy Smart Gang were after the Doctor, surely they should be on his side. Meanwhile, Polly stared at what Sam was standing on and gazed around the cellar.

"An electrical circuit," she exclaimed, with a flash of inspiration. "Where's the note we found in the study? It tells us how to open the door."

Can you work out how to open the door?

29

Dr Perry-Ment Explains

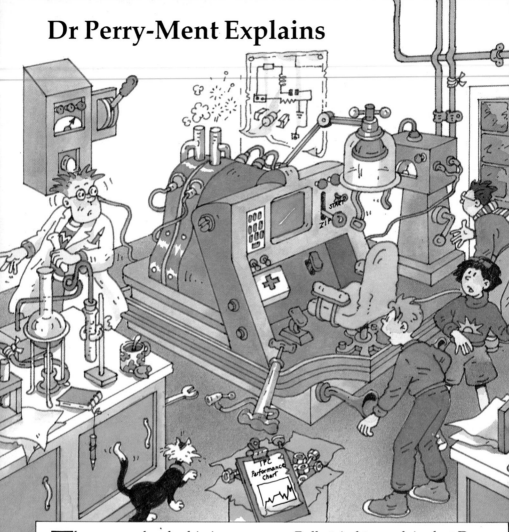

There was a loud whirring sound and several clicks. The door slowly opened and they stepped through into a laboratory. At first, no one noticed the eccentric figure half hidden by a peculiar machine. But he had seen them.

"I know who you are," he said, looking alarmed. "You're working for the Smart Gang."

Polly tried to explain, but Dr Perry-Ment was still suspicious. If only they could prove they were nothing to do with the Gang. Suddenly Sam remembered. He did have something which belonged to the Doctor. If he gave it back, Perry-Ment would know they weren't working for the Smarts.

What has Sam got?

"Now I know you're on my side you can help me to spook the Smarts away," the Doctor said.

Joe, Polly and Sam looked a bit puzzled as the Doctor began to explain.

I am a scientist and I was working on a top-secret project when I made an amazing discovery...

... an incredible invention. But one of the junior scientists was working for the evil Smart Gang and they plotted to steal it.

I inherited the Manor 12 years ago, just as my granny had told me when I was a small boy.

What could I do alone? A bodyguard will be here tomorrow, but in the meantime I decided to frighten the Gang by dressing up as a ghost. Now you're here it will be much easier.

The Manor seemed a perfect hiding place. I moved in and set up my laboratory here. My invention is a machine that moves people from place to place, instantly.

I call it the IPT and it is working well. But so far, it will only move in Internal Mode.

Five days ago, I spotted figures outside; a face at the window. The Smart Gang had found me.

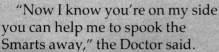

The IPT Machine

Polly and Joe looked doubtful. The Doctor's plan sounded crazy. But it was their only chance to outsmart the Smarts and help Perry-Ment. First, they would need some ghost outfits.

"The Gang are searching the house again. We'll surprise them in the Games Room," the Doctor said, hurrying off to the attic with Polly. "See you there."

Polly dug out an old white dress from the dressing-up box. She pulled it on and covered herself with smelly white powder.

Sam tried on the Doctor's ghost outfit. He had to make a few alterations to make it fit, but he thought he looked very spooky in the end. The first aid box gave Joe an idea. It took him ages to unwind all the bandages and wind them around himself, but he decided it would make a brilliant fancy dress.

At last they were ready. It was then that they realized they were trapped. The only door was the secret one they had come in by and neither could see how to open it from this side.

"I know," exclaimed Sam. "We'll use the machine."

But how did it work? Sam pulled the START lever. Instructions flashed onto the screen. He had seen the ZIP stick but what was the ZAP number? There weren't any numbers on the machine. Suddenly he gasped. In the screen he could see a face… the ghost! He watched in horror as it's arm reached out towards him.

But the ghost was trying to help them. It pointed at a book which was the IPT handbook. As they began to read, they realized they could work out the ZAP number and which keys to press on the machine.

What is the ZAP number? Which keys should they press?

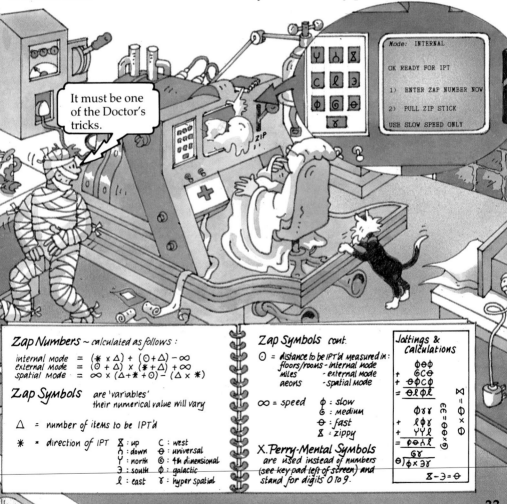

It must be one of the Doctor's tricks.

Mode: INTERNAL

OK READY FOR IPT

1) ENTER ZAP NUMBER NOW

2) PULL ZIP STICK

USE SLOW SPEED ONLY

Zap Numbers ~ calculated as follows :

internal mode = $(\ast \times \triangle) + (\odot + \triangle) - \infty$
external mode = $(\odot + \triangle) \times (\ast + \triangle) + \infty$
spatial mode = $\infty \times (\triangle + \ast + \odot) - (\triangle \times \ast)$

Zap Symbols are 'variables' their numerical value will vary

$\triangle$ = number of items to be IPT'd

$\ast$ = direction of IPT

४ : up	C : west
ᚻ : down	↺ : universal
Y : north	⑥ : 4th dimensional
Ɛ : south	φ : galactic
ℓ : east	૪ : hyper spatial

Zap Symbols cont.

$\odot$ = distance to be IPT'd measured in :
floors/rooms - internal mode
miles - external mode
aeons - spatial mode

∞ = speed
φ : slow
ϭ : medium
θ : fast
४ : zippy

X.Perry-Mental Symbols are used instead of numbers (see key pad left of screen) and stand for digits 0 to 9.

Jottings & Calculations

φθφ
+ ϭCθ
+ θφCφ
= θℓφℓ

Φ४४
+ ℓφ४
+ YYℓ
= φθλℓ

ϭ४
θ√φ×Ɛ४

४-Ɛ=θ

Ghostly Tricks

The machine whirred, buzzed and rattled. It finally shuddered to a stop in a cloud of green smoke. Sam blinked. With a start he realized they were in the library. Joe tapped in the ZAP number and sent the machine back to the laboratory.

Polly and Perry-Ment were hard at work in the games room. The Doctor was brushing florescent paint onto plastic skulls which made them glow eerily in the gloom and Polly was trying out a trick she had read about with dried peas, a glass and a metal tray.

Sam had an idea. He and Polly could be a headless ghost. He found her a black hood and then dashed behind a black curtain. As he balanced on a stool with his head tucked under Polly's arm, he tried to ask the Doctor about the ghostly figure.

My uncle used to put on magic shows here so there are lots of props.

The peas at the bottom swell and push out the ones on top. So they rattle down onto the tray and make a spooky noise.

But the Doctor was busy. He had decided to try an old trick from his uncle's book using a special chair and a mirror. His head was supposed to look as if it was floating in midair. But although he read and reread the instructions, he couldn't make it work. Finally he gave up.

Meanwhile, Polly and Sam had discovered a large mirror at the back of the stage with a lever to tilt it.

"Pepper's Ghost," exclaimed the Doctor. "That's one trick that will work."

He told Joe to jump into the pit and stand below the floodlight where he couldn't be seen. Sam was to carry on tilting the top of the mirror down towards the stage.

What will the audience see?

In Search of the Smart Gang

They ran to their ghostly
positions as footsteps grew
louder and closer. There were
voices in the library, but they
faded away as the steps carried on
downstairs.

"There's someone in the hall,"
hissed Sam. "They're coming this
way."

They came closer and closer...
but no. They too carried on past.

"We'll just have to go after
them," exclaimed Dr X. Perry-
Ment.

Joe and the Doctor hurried into
the library while Polly and Sam
ran into the hall.

They tiptoed around the rest of
the floor, peering cautiously into
each room, but they found no
one. Suddenly a board creaked
behind them. Polly froze, then
sighed with relief when she
looked back. It was only the cat.

"Let's look downstairs," she said, feeling braver.

They crept down and stopped. Voices coming from the drawing room! This was scary.

What were they supposed to do now? Sam gulped and turned the handle slowly. There was silence on the other side of the door.

"Come on," Polly croaked.

They flung open the door and leapt into the room, trying to look as frightening as possible. BANG, CRASH, THUD. They collided with two other, very solid ghosts… Joe and the Doctor.

"This is useless," said Joe, picking himself up.

"We'll never scare the Gang like this," he added.

"Wait a minute," exclaimed Polly. "What's the time? I think I know where we can find all four Gang members together."

Where will they find the Gang?

Spooking the Smarts

The Doctor led the way to an incredible octagonal ballroom which was lined from floor to ceiling with mirrors. He held up his hand in front of one of the panels. It slid open and they stepped into a small, secret room, where they could hide and wait for the Gang. The walls were one-way windows and they could watch the ballroom. Although it was impossible to see into the room from outside.

The last to arrive was a sinister-looking girl wearing dark glasses. She seemed to be the boss.

"Well?" she snapped at the other three who looked very sheepish. "Have you found anything yet?"

Now was their chance. The Doctor released the panel. The four "ghosts" leaped out and the panel slid silently shut.

The Gang looked surprised, but not a bit frightened. Then suddenly the spy called Rex gasped. Seconds later, all four Gang members took to their heels. Looks of utter terror were on their faces.

Why? Joe and Polly were puzzled. Then Joe caught sight of something. Now he understood.

What frightened the Gang?

The Ghost in the Mirror

The ghost chased after the Gang, hovering in midair, howling. Joe, Polly, Sam and Perry-Ment raced after them. They reached the hall in time to see Rex cowering, petrified, by the front door.

He was desperately trying to open it. But at last he gave up and ran after the rest of the Smarts. With the ghost in hot pursuit, the Gang dashed along the corridor and straight on through the drawing room.

"Let me out of here!" yelled Rex, running into the dining room.

Joe and Polly watched from the door as the Smarts fumbled with one of the barred windows. The boss was already halfway through.

Seconds later, the last of the Gang climbed out. Polly, Sam and Joe ran into the room and watched incredulously as the ghost melted back into the mirror. Sam was sure the phantom smiled as it began to fade away.

"That's got rid of them," exclaimed Joe, watching the creepy quartet race away.

Sam stared at the mirror where the ghost had vanished. There was one final question.

Who was the ghost in the mirror? The Doctor smiled mysteriously. It was someone he knew very well. Polly thought she knew the answer.

Who is the ghost in the mirror?

Clues

Pages 6-7
Is there an open window? They can use the rope and hook.

Pages 8-9
Look for something to help them find their way around the house.

Pages 10-11
The window with the green light is on the second floor.

Pages 12-13
Think backwards.

Pages 14-15
Where do the footprints lead? Look at the book titles on page 12.

Pages 16-17
Try exchanging the last letter of the first word with the first letter of the second word.

Pages 18-19
This is easy. Use your eyes.

Pages 20-21
Use your eyes again.

Pages 22-23
Flip back through the book.

Pages 24-25
A different code is used on each document. Extra letters have been added to one.

Pages 26-27
Look at the map again. Where are they? Can you spot a hidden door?

Pages 28-29
Look at the note on page 13.

Pages 30-31
Has Sam picked anything up recently?

Pages 32-33
Hint:
Number of persons = 2
Direction = 9 (up)
Distance in floors = 2 (cellars to first floor)
Speed = 1 (slow)

Work out which X. Perry-Mental symbols stand for which numbers by solving the sums in the handbook.

Pages 34-35
Think hard and use your imagination.

Pages 36-37
Look at the mirror message on page 17. What is the time?

Pages 38-39
Look carefully at everyone in the ballroom and their reflections.

Pages 40-41
Look at the paintings and the family tree on page 11.

Answers

Pages 6-7

Using the pole with the hook, they pull down both ends of the rope pulley. The rope is hooked around the tire and Joe sits in it, holding the pole. Polly and Sam hoist him up until he is level with the open window. He then hooks the pole on the window bar and swings himself inside. The tire is lowered and Polly is hoisted up by Sam. Joe holds out the pole and drags her in. He then pulls in the free end of the rope using the pole. Polly and Joe lower the tire again and then haul Sam up, again using the pole to drag him inside.

Tire   Pole with hook   Rope pulley   Open window

Pages 8-9

Polly has spotted a guide and map to Grimstone Manor.

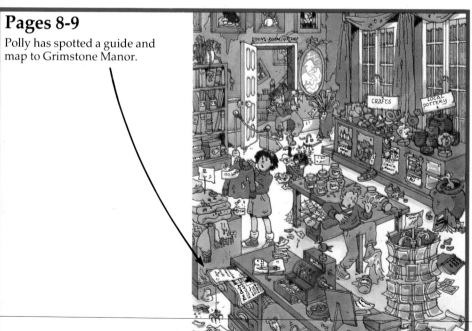

Pages 10-11

They should go to the study on the second floor which was where the strange glow came from on the previous night.

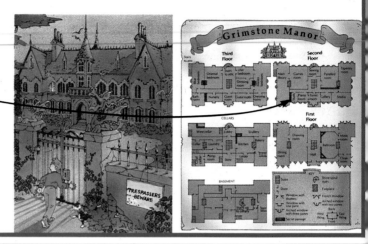

Pages 12-13

The note is written backwards. This is what it says with punctuation added:

To go from the dark to my secret cellar, look for the bottles and take out the Mellier. Press for the wine and press for the door, push right down or you will get no more. A glass on a bottle not a bottle by a glass. Place the jugs on the circle and then you will pass.

Remember

Pages 14-15

The footsteps go towards the bookcase which is the secret door. The handle is the book called HANDEL by I.M.A Lever.

Hidden lever

Footprints

Pages 16-17

The message is decoded by swapping the last letter of each word with the first letter of the next. It says:

Search everywhere. The lab must be found. The machine will be mine. Meeting 15:30 hours, ballroom. The Boss. Code X

Pages 18-19

Joe is right. He has spotted the rear view of the ghost in the mirror, which clearly shows someone wearing a ghost costume.

Pages 20-21

The fireplace has changed which suggests it is a secret, revolving door and that there are two fireplaces.

The differences are ringed here.

Pages 22-23

They saw the girl standing outside Grimstone Manor on page 6.

Pages 24-25

The first document has one extra letter (or number) added in front of each group of letters. It is decoded by taking away the first dud letter and then amending the spacing to make words. It says:

THE SMART GANG DOSSIER 1

FACTS KNOWN

Name: Dr Xavier Perry-Ment

Born: 4 December 1950

Moved into Grimstone Manor in early September. Under Smart Gang surveillance since 10 September. World famous scientist working on top secret invention – Instant Physical Transference machine. Uses his own special code to work the machine in which symbols equal digits 0-9. Smarts still working to break code. He also sometimes uses a word code for his notes.

Code K

Pages 24-25 (continued)

The second document is decoded by swapping the first and last letters of each word. It says:

SMART GANG DOSSIER 2

Gang's uses for the machine:

could be rented to other crooks; entry to bank vaults, museums and galleries (and quick exits with loot leaving no trace); entry to government offices.

Operation Perry-Ment commences 12:00 hours on Saturday 24 September.

Code T

Pages 26-27

The map on page 10 shows a stone spiral staircase leading from the basement up to the cellars. This is in the room directly below the kitchen. You can see the hinges and edge of a trapdoor hidden below the rug where Polly, Joe and Sam are hiding.

Trapdoor

Pages 28-29

The door is opened by completing an electrical circuit. Polly works out how to do this from the coded note they found in the study on page 13.

They have to:

1) Remove the wine bottle labelled Mellier;
2) Press the wine press down;
3) Find the bottle with a glass on the label and take away the bottle and glass next to it;
4) Place the eight jugs on the dark stone slabs. (There are contact points on the slabs and also on the bottom of the jugs.) Sam is standing on the battery which powers the circuit.

Contact points

Take these away

Wine press

Battery

46

Pages 30-31

Sam has Dr Perry-Ment's plan of the IPT motor. When the Smarts were returning on page 26, he crammed the yellow plan into his pocket without thinking. It is still in his pocket on page 29 in the wine cellar.

Page 26

We'll pick up the file. I don't know how you forgot it.

Yeah – then we'll find those snooping brats.

The plan

Page 29

Pages 32-33

There are ten X. Perry-Mental Symbols and each one stands for a different number from 0-9. You can decode all the symbols by working out the Doctor's simple sums scribbled in the margin of the handbook.

X. Perry-Mental Symbols:

୪	φ	⑥	⊖	c	ℓ	϶	Ϥ	ɦ	Ҳ
0	1	2	3	4	5	6	7	8	9

The handbook shows the formulae for three Zap Numbers. The correct formula depends on the machine's Mode. The screen display shows the machine is operating in Internal Mode and says to use Slow Speed only.

The symbols used in the formula are explained in the list of Zap Symbols. The numbers they represent vary, but for Joe and Sam's move they are as follows:

Numerical value of each variable Zap Symbol:		X. Perry-Mental Symbols
number of people	= 2 (Joe and Sam)	⑥
direction	= 9 (up)	Ҳ
distance in floors	= 2 (cellar to first floor)	⑥
speed	= 1 (slow)	φ

So the equation to find the Zap Number is:

$$(9 \times 2) + (2 \times 2) - 1 = 21$$

The Zap Number is 21 and in X. Perry-Mental Symbols this is ⑥φ. These are the keys which Sam must press.

Pages 34-35

Pepper's Ghost is a famous trick. If Joe stands down in the pit so he can't be seen and the mirror is tilted, his image will be projected up onto the stage. The audience then see a ghostly image appear.

The diagram shows how Pepper's Ghost works.

Pages 36-37

They will find the Gang in the ballroom at 3:30 p.m. (15:30 hours).

The mirror message on page 17 is from The Boss, the leader of the Smart Gang and it arranges the meeting. Dr Perry-Ment's watch shows the time is now 3:20 p.m. They still have time to reach the ballroom before the Gang members arrive.

Pages 38-39

Polly, Joe, Sam and the Doctor are all reflected in the mirrors, but there is one extra ghostly figure who has no reflection. This must be a real ghost.

The real ghost

Pages 40-41

The ghost is Mathilda, the Doctor's grandmother. Her portrait is in the family tree on page 11 and there is also a painting of her in the dining room. When you first see the portrait, Mathilda is frowning, but in the final picture her portrait is smiling after frightening away the Gang.

The ghost

The portraits ... before and after

Mathilda

Before

After

First published in 1989 by
Usborne Publishing Ltd,
83-85 Saffron Hill,
London EC1N 8RT, England.

Copyright © 1989 Usborne Publishing Ltd.

The name Usborne and the device ♆ are Trade Marks of Usborne Publishing Ltd.

Printed in Italy.   American edition 19